VARLEY

Graveyard dirt /

DEMON SLAYER
GRAVEYARD DIRT

by Dax Varley
illustrated by Jon Proctor

Spellbound

An Imprint of Magic Wagon
abdopublishing.com

Huge thanks to Julie Pitzel, Bob Mann, Vicki Sansum, and Lenny Enderle. —DV

For Jewell —JP

abdopublishing.com

Printed in the United States of America, North Mankato, Minnesota.
022016
092016

THIS BOOK CONTAINS
RECYCLED MATERIALS

Written by Dax Varley
Illustrated by Jon Proctor
Edited by Tamara L. Britton and Megan M. Gunderson
Designed by Candice Keimig

Cataloging-in-Publication Data

Names: Varley, Dax, author. | Proctor, Jon, illustrator.
Title: Graveyard dirt / by Dax Varley ; illustrated by Jon Proctor.
Description: Minneapolis, MN : Magic Wagon, [2017] | Series: Demon slayer ; #2
Summary: After more women go missing, Max continues his search for his mother and his study of demons who took her.
Identifiers: LCCN 2016934393 | ISBN 9781624021589 (lib. bdg.) | ISBN 9781680790085 (ebook)
Subjects: LCSH: Mothers and sons¬--Fiction. | Kidnapping--Fiction. | Demonology--Fiction.
Classification: DDC [Fic]--dc23
LC record available at http://lccn.loc.gov/2016934393

TABLE OF CONTENTS

CHAPTER 1

FOLLOW, FOLLOW

"Another woman's been **TAKEN**," Dad said. He showed me the news headline.

I read what I could from my spot at the breakfast table. "Same way as Mom."

Dad nodded. "Yep. Right down to the red **HAIR**." He rubbed his forehead, weary. "Who would do this?"

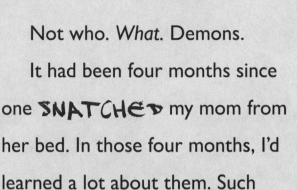

Not who. *What.* Demons.

It had been four months since one SNATCHED my mom from her bed. In those four months, I'd learned a lot about them. Such nasty little **boogers**.

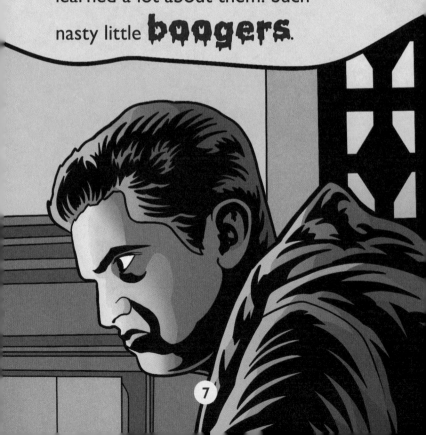

7

Here's the thing about
demons: they are everywhere and
nowhere. Some are lone. Some live in
tribes. Some are shape-shifters.
Some **possess** the living.

The ones that look human are hard to detect. But the ones that look like *DEMONS* are easy to find.

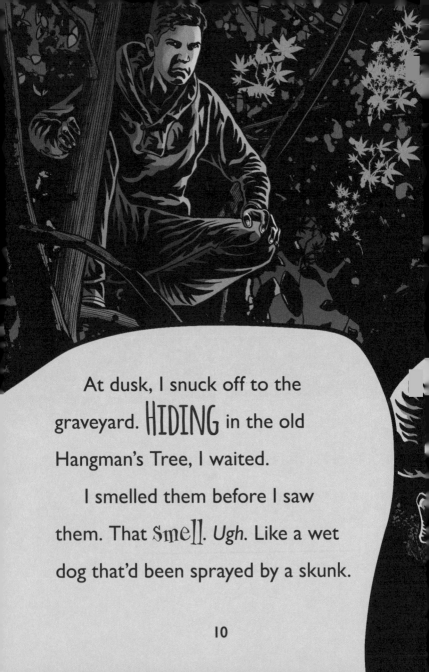

At dusk, I snuck off to the graveyard. HIDING in the old Hangman's Tree, I waited.

I smelled them before I saw them. That smell. *Ugh.* Like a wet dog that'd been sprayed by a skunk.

I readied my slingshot. It'd be so easy to pick them off . . . one, two, three.

I knew only one way to kill demons—shoot them with game tokens from Sonny's Arcade. It wasn't the shape or the metal that took the devils down. It was the *emblem* on the back. A sunburst.

Sunbursts represent light. Ancient cultures used them to ward off evil.

The tokens were perfect ammo. And for an added punch, I soaked them overnight in *witch hazel*.

I had to be careful though. If I slayed them all, I'd never find Mom. My plan was to wait and follow.

CHAPTER 2

BULLIES

I heard **rustling** from behind a tombstone. A small demon inched forward. He *dragged* his right foot like it'd been snapped at the ankle. Compared to the others, he looked like a runt. Was it a child?

The other demons paused their dirt gobbling. The lame one moved toward them. **Step** . . . *drag* . . . **step** . . . *drag.*

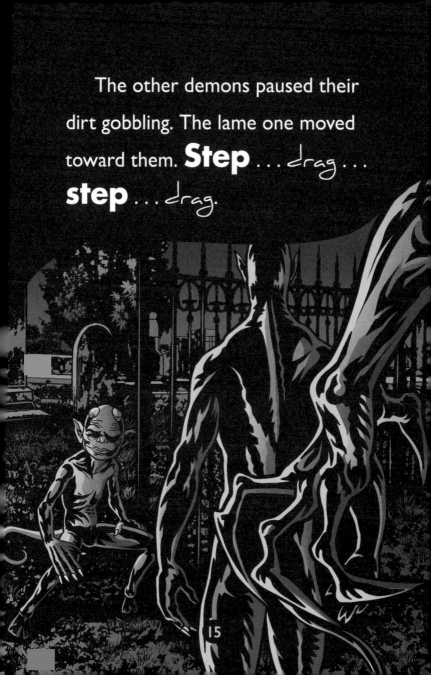

I lowered my slingshot, totally amazed.

The runt neared the others. Then he dropped to his knees and scooped up a handful of dirt.

The others watched for a moment. Then whip-snap, they **RAGED**. Baring their fangs, they **pounced**, kicking and clawing the lame one.

17

Jumping jackalopes! These monsters even bully their own.

I raised my slingshot and took aim. Whap! Whap! Whap! The three bully demons exploded in puffs of dust, their bits raining down on their *prey*.

19

The little guy tried to make a break for it. But I dropped down from the branch and ran for him. I pulled the canteen from my belt and sprinkled him with witch hazel. He fell, **SCREAMING**.

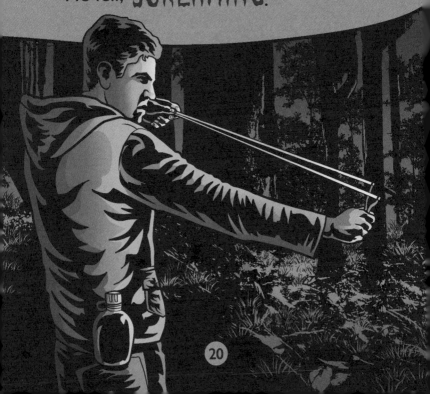

"Where's my mother?" I demanded, my SLINGSHOT pulled tight over him.

"I can't tell you," he whimpered.

I poured a stream of witch hazel on his ear and listened to it *SIZZLE*. "Can you tell me now, or should I burn the other ear off too?"

"If I tell you, they'll kill me."

"If you don't, *I'll* kill you."

He curled into a ball and cried. I almost felt sorry for him. *Almost.* He was a *DEMON*, after all.

He sniffled. "She's underground."

"Underground where?"

"I can't tell you," he said. "But I can show you."

"Even better." I stared at him hard. "As long as it's not a trick."

"No trick. Just *please*," he
begged, "don't hurt me anymore."

Risky? Yes. But I had to
chance it. Was I really this close to
getting Mom back?

CHAPTER 3

WAILING WOODS

I followed him, weapons ready.

Step . . . drag . . . **step** . . . drag.

Ugh. Of all the demons to lead me.

This one would lose a snail race.

I thought about carrying

him piggyback, but even *his* tiny

CLAWS could still puncture a

hole in my head.

After an **ETERNITY**, we took
a path on the right. I knew the area.
We call it the Wailing Woods.
Supposedly, two boy scouts
got caught in quicksand here. And
people say you can still hear their
ghosts **WAILING** for help.

Deeper in, the runt moved toward an old torn-up cabin. He pointed. "There."

"In there?" I asked.

He shook his head. "No, *down* there. In the storm cellar."

I gave him a **shove**. "Show me."

His eyes welled up again. "If they find out, they'll kill me."

"Like I care."

"Please. I helped you."

The little beast had a point. I really just wanted my mom back. But maybe I could **RESCUE** the other women, too.

I nodded toward the canteen
tucked in my belt. "Go on then,
before I **drown** you in this stuff."
He started hobbling off.

The runt hadn't lied. There was a storm cellar in the back. I raised the door and peered in.

Gag! Demon ODOR. Heavy traces. But I heard nothing down there.

I took out my flashlight and shone it down. "Mom?"

Silence.

"Mom?" I called louder.

It had to be a trick. The place was quieter than the graveyard. But what if Mom couldn't answer? What if they had **gagged** her?

I placed the flashlight between my teeth and readied my slingshot. The steps CREAKED under my weight. I flashed the light around the cellar.

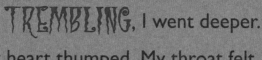 **TREMBLING**, I went deeper. My heart thumped. My throat felt like an hourglass full of sand.

I reached the bottom. All clear. Or so I thought.

CHAPTER 4

BE PREPARED

Demon Number One bolted out from under the staircase. I aimed my slingshot, but Demon Number Two popped up from behind some crates. He kicked me from behind. I landed face first on the FILTHY wooden floor.

Both demons jumped me.
CLAWS ripped into my heavy
jacket and jeans. My warm blood
oozed.

The slingshot was out of reach,
and I couldn't get to the witch hazel.
But still, I'd come prepared.

I scrambled up and—*jab!*—
knocked Demon One in the chin
with my fist. He burst like a balloon.
Demon Two got a roundhouse hook
in the jaw. *POP!* He vanished too.

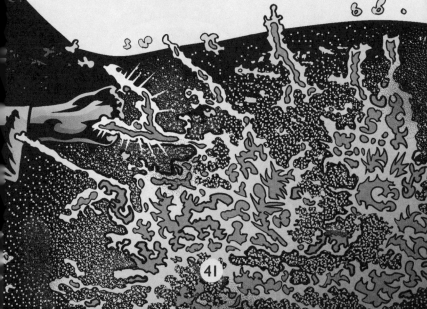

I staggered back, adjusting the ring on my finger. It wasn't just any ring. I'd made it with a witch hazel-soaked token, sunburst side up.

I gathered my things and stumbled up the stairs. I was bleeding badly.

Guess who I saw just peeking around the cabin? "You set me up!" I shouted, charging the runt.

His *DEMON EYES* popped wide and he tried to rush off. No contest. I nailed him, pinning him to the ground. "Where is she?"

He flashed a **wicked** grin. "She's ours, Max. You'll never get her back."

I raised my fist. I wanted to crush my token ring right through his face.

"Go ahead. Kill me. I know you want to."

"Answer one thing. Why her?"

He turned his head away, **REFUSING** to answer. Or maybe waiting for me to do him in.

I was **losing** both blood and strength. I dropped my fist. "You're not worth the energy." I stood. "Get out of here."

He pulled himself up and limped off. **Step** . . . *drag* . . . **step** . . . *drag*. Before disappearing into the trees, he turned. What he called back sent spidery chills up my spine.

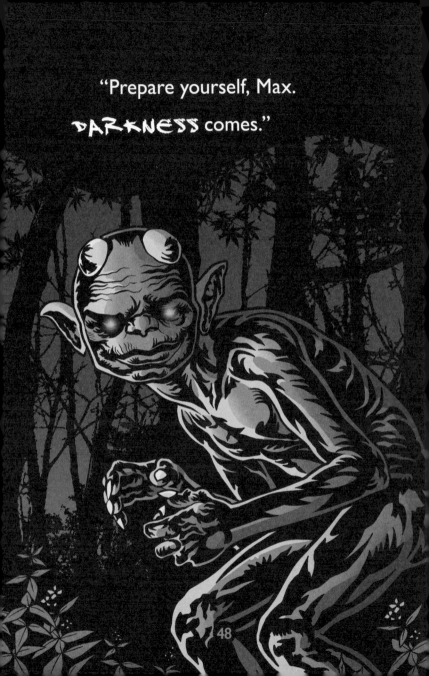